MEG'S VEG

for Sam

MEG'S VEG

by Helen Nicoll
and Jan Pieńkowski

PUFFIN BOOKS

It was springtime. Time for Meg
to start her vegetable garden

Meg fetched the muck

Owl
sowed
peas
and
carrots

Mog
put in
a
pumpkin

Meg
sowed
some
seeds
she
had
found
in
her
cauldron

It was so cold, no seeds grew

Mog
made
a
scarecrow
to
guard
his
pumpkin

BRRRR

Meg
tried
to
make
the
sun
shine

Make a
sunshine
spell

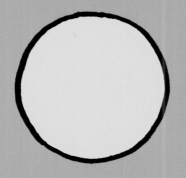

and
hotter

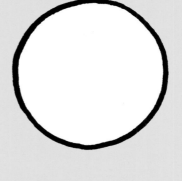

and
hotter

The rain came down in sheets

They had

They
made
a
huge
compost
heap

Then
they
had to
stake
the
peas

They had to hoe down the rows

and water the pumpkin

And then,
they
had to
eat
them
all

Goodbye!